TALES FROM THE OLD WORLD

Kevin Crossley-Holland

First published in Great Britain 2000
by
Dolphin
a division of the Orion Publishing
Group Ltd
This Large Print edition published by
BBC Audiobooks Ltd
by arrangement with
Orion
2004

ISBN 0 7540 7938 4

British Library Cataloguing in Publication Data

Crossley-Holland, Kevin
  Tales from the old world.—New ed., Large print ed
  1. Folklore—Europe—Juvenile literature 2. Tales—
  Europe—Juvenile literature 3. Large type books
  I. Title
  398.2'094[J]

ISBN 0-7540-7938-4

Printed and bound in Great Britain by
Antony Rowe Ltd., Chippenham, Wiltshire

For my daughters
OENONE and ELEANOR

CONTENTS

FOREWORD

The beauty and beast of language! As sharp as the most subtle thoughts and feelings we are capable of; as crude as a bludgeon.

A 'family of nations' is one of those phrases that has been blunted by overuse. But think about it. Doesn't it suggest people of different nationalities who are closely or distantly related by blood, the roots of their language, history, tradition and common concern? It makes sense to call the Europeans a family of nations, fond of squabbling or fighting, but always part of each other's stories, living cheek by jowl on the same continent.

This book is a kind of sampler of the tales which relate Europeans more deeply than the European Union. Here are myths that illustrate why tides ebb and flow and why the seasons turn, and the legend of King Arthur, celebrated as a hero throughout medieval Europe.

ix

Here, too, are people like you and me and our next-door neighbours, coming to some crossing-place in their lives, and folk-tales involving giants and little people, a supernatural cow, an ugly duckling and a whole army of bears.

Europeans called their homelands the Old World after colonizing the New World of North America. But here's a paradox: these ten old stories from the Old World make our old world new! Why not read them and see? Yes, and thanks for reading this.

I'll say that again. Danke schon. Danke schön. Mange tek. Bedankt. Dukuji. Dànk u wéll. Kiitos. Efharisto. Thanks!

Kevin Crossley-Holland
Burnham Market, August 1999

THE PIED PIPER OF HAMELIN

Rats! There was a ruin of rats. A rat-attack! A plague of rats. Sidling along streets; scavenging in shops; high-tailing around houses. No one in Hamelin knew what to do about them.

To begin with, there were only a few more than usual. As if the town-rats had simply invited their friends from upriver and downriver to come and have a look round Hamelin.

But then there were a lot more than usual, as if all those friends had decided to stay on, and before long invited their friends . . .

People began to complain. They didn't like the sight of them, always scurrying round corners, or the smell of them, so sour and strong. And they didn't like the sound of them, squeaking and scritching-and-scratching in every single house.

How fast they were on their feet! They bit the hind-legs of dogs ten times their size; they buried their teeth in the

1

throats of cats; and they actually nipped babies in their cradles.

From the corners of kitchens, they grinned at cooks and then sprang up and licked their soup-ladles; they nose-dived under larder doors, and gnawed their way into the casks of salted sprat and salted herring; they chewed the rims of cheeses; then they curled up their tails, and nested inside men's Sunday hats. Rats! There was a ruin of rats. A rat-attack! A plague of rats.

At last the people of Hamelin marched to the Town Hall. They were shouting. They were chanting. They were carrying banners with words painted on them: RATS OUT! and I SMELL A RAT; and also, more worryingly for the Mayor, I SMELL A MAYOR.

The Mayor wasn't a rat. He was such a knickerbockered dumpling he couldn't have scampered anywhere to save his life; and his eyes weren't small or beady but large and grey and somehow faded; but he did have a fur coat—a brown velvet gown lined with white ermine. And so did all the

2

councillors.

'We paid for those gowns,' shouted one man.

'And we'll have them off your backs,' called another.

'Rats! What are you going to do about them?'

'Get rid of them!'

'You're useless!'

'Disgraceful!'

The Mayor and the councillors could see that, unless they got rid of the rats, they would never be elected again. But what were they to do? The town ratcatcher had laid traps and sprinkled poison and, true, he had caught a few dozen rats. But you can't catch a whole army any more than you can catch a rainstorm in a pail. So what were they to do?

For more than an hour the Mayor and councillors sat in council.

They sat in silence and rocked to and fro and racked their brains.

'Oh! My head aches,' said the Mayor. 'It's all very well. All very well!'

At noon, the Mayor's stomach invited him to stop thinking about rats.

It told him it was time to think about a large bowl of thick green turtle soup.

'Good idea!' murmured the Mayor, and his eyes brightened.

At that moment, there was a gentle but firm rat-a-tat-tat at the great oak door of the council chamber.

The Mayor gave a start. 'Oh dear!' he said, and he fanned himself with his right hand. 'Anything like that and— and I think it's a rat.' Using his elbows, the Mayor levered himself upright in his carved Mayoral chair. 'Come in!' he cried.

In came the strangest-looking figure. In and straight up to the Mayor. He was wrapped in a gown so long he could have trapped its hem under his heels, and this gown was half yellow and half red: a marvel, a swaying jigsaw of crescents and diamonds, full-moons and coffins and zigzags and squares.

The man himself was tall and thin, with green and blue eyes. He had one of those seamless, hairless, almost ageless faces, and might have been thirty or fifty or even seventy years old.

The man smiled at the Mayor and,

4

so it seemed to them, at each of the councillors—little, quick elfin smiles.

'Please, your honours,' said the man. 'Please and listen.'

'Go on!' said the Mayor.

'And hurry up about it, man!' said the Mayor's stomach.

'I may be able to help you,' said the man. 'I have a special skill! I can make every creature under the sun follow me.'

'Follow you?' said the Mayor.

'Every creature that creeps or runs or swims or flies. I've led away armies of moles and toads and vipers. Do you understand?'

'I follow you,' said the Mayor.

'And people call me the Pied Piper,' said the man, holding up his hands and trilling his fingers.

Then for the first time the Mayor and councillors of Hamelin noticed that the man was wearing a red-and-yellow sash round his neck, with a little reed pipe dangling from it.

'You see!' said the man, smiling. 'Now please and listen! Last June I saved the Cham of Tartary from a terrible swarm of gnats.'

'You did?' said the councillors.

'They were whining around his whiskers,' said the Piper.

'Pickled pepper!' said the Mayor.

'And in Asia,' said the Piper, 'I rescued the Nizam from a brood of vampire-bats. So as you see: I can rid Hamelin of your plague of rats.'

'You can?' said the Mayor. 'How much? I mean: how much?'

'One thousand guilders.'

'One thousand!' exclaimed the Mayor. 'One! We'll give you fifty thousand—and cheap at the price.'

The Piper smiled another little, quick smile and bowed. Then he sailed out of the Town Hall, followed by the Mayor and the councillors. Down in the street, the Piper waited until quite a crowd had gathered around him, curious to see what he would do. Then he raised his reed pipe and pursed his lips; his blue-green eyes were dancing.

As soon as the Piper began to play, there was a far-off sound, like a sound at the back of your mind, or the sound of the distant sea. But this hum became a mutter, and the mutter a grumble, and the grumble a rumble, as rats jumped down from barrels and ran along rafters and drummed over floorboards and tumbled downstairs, hundreds of rats, thousands of them, all eager to join the dance.

There were black rats and brown rats and some black-and-tans. Mothers and fathers and squeaking friskers. Grey-faced grandparents. Thick-waisted uncles and stern aunts with whiskers!

The Piper advanced from street to street, and he never stopped piping, not for one moment. He danced the rats all the way round Hamelin and then he led them down to the river. The Piper walked straight into the water and the rats followed him. They all dived in and drowned in the River Weser—all except one.

This one rat swam right across the river. He ran back to Ratland, and when he got there, he told the other rats: 'That music! What music! When the Piper started to play, I heard a sigh of bread rising in the oven and the hiss of fresh milk squirting into the pail;

I heard the seething of damson jam; I heard corks popping and bacon crackling; I heard bubble-and-squeak! I heard a sweet, sweet voice telling me to eat and drink and eat—and at that moment, I found myself up to my neck in cold water.'

Then all the people of Hamelin began to gather in the market-place and the church bells rang. They rang and rang until the steeple rocked.

The Mayor was purple in the face with pleasure. 'Get sticks!' he shouted. 'Get long poles! Poke out their holy nests! Block up their poky holes! I don't want a trace of them left in Hamelin.'

Then the Piper sauntered into the market-place. 'But first, your honour,' he said, 'please and pay me my one thousand guilders.'

'One thousand guilders!' exclaimed the Mayor, and he turned from purple to blue.

'One thousand!' murmured the councillors. 'We can't afford a thousand. What about our council dinners?'

'Mmm!' murmured the Mayor. 'We could buy a butt of Rhine wine for half that amount.'

'And then there's the claret and the Graves and the Moselle.'

'Exactly!' said the Mayor. He rubbed his nose and then he winked at the councillors. 'Well!' he said. 'The rats are drowned and dead, and the dead can't come back to life, can they!' The Mayor wagged a finger at the Piper. 'A thousand indeed! We were only joking, and you know it. But fair's fair: we'll give you a decent bottle, and here—take fifty guilders!'

'Don't you play around with me!' said the Piper, and his eyes shone blue and green, like candle-flames sprinkled with salt. 'I'm in a hurry. I've promised to be in Baghdad in time for supper.'

'Baghdad!' cried the Mayor.

'The caliph's cook is making me a bowl of his best stew. I rid his kitchen of a nest of scorpions, and that's all he can afford.'

The Mayor turned puce. He began to fan himself with his right hand.

'I didn't drive a hard bargain with

him,' said the Piper, 'but I won't let you off—not one penny. And I'll tell you this: if you anger me, I'll pipe another kind of tune.'

'Are you telling me you've charged that cook a bowl of stew, and you're asking us for a thousand guilders?' demanded the Mayor. 'I'm not going to be insulted by you—you piebald gypsy! How dare you threaten me? You can blow on your pipe until you balloon! Blow until you burst!'

The Piper raised his reed pipe and pursed his lips; and before he had blown three notes, there was a far-off sound, like the sound of wind in the high tree-tops. But this rustling became a bustling, and the bustling a hustling, as dozens and dozens of children burst into the market-place. Scampering and skipping and shouting and laughing, they thronged around the Piper, all of them eager to join the dance.

There were boys. There were girls. Brothers, half-brothers, sisters, step-sisters. There were little tiny creatures, who had only just learned to walk. And last, a moon-faced boy, whose right leg was all crooked.

Then the Piper stepped out of the market-place, and he never stopped piping, not for one moment. Hopping and clapping, quickstepping, chattering, the children of Hamelin followed him. Their clogs clattered on the cobblestones.

But the Mayor and the councillors: they were spell-bound. The magical music that made the children dance and sing silenced them and rooted them to the spot. They couldn't move; they couldn't even shout warnings.

The Pied Piper danced the children all the way round Hamelin and then, to the terror of the Mayor and councillors, he led them down to the river.

The Weser slipped and slapped against its banks. It sang happy and sad, it echoed the death-songs of all the drowned rats.

Right at the water's edge, the Piper turned aside. He set off along the path on the river-bank, and all the children danced after him. They left Hamelin behind, and crossed the July meadows, and reached the foot of basking Koppelberg.

The hill was steep, the path was steep. But just as it seemed the Piper and children could climb no further, a green door swung open in the side of the hill. The Piper didn't pause. No! With a little, quick smile he walked straight in, and all the children of Hamelin stepped in after him.

All? All except one. The boy with the crooked leg couldn't dance. He was still way below, calling out to his friends, dragging himself up the stony path.

Then the green door swung shut again, and the moon-faced boy was left on the hillside. He stared and stared; then he folded on to his hands and knees.

* * *

The spluttering Mayor and councillors sent town messengers north and south and east and west, with instructions to offer the Piper as much silver and gold as he wanted, if only he would bring the children back to Hamelin. But where had he gone? Where were the children? Time passed.

The men and women of Hamelin wept for their sons and daughters. They named the track that runs along the river-bank Pied Piper Street. They cut a story in stone. They painted a church window. Time passed.

*   *   *

Time passed and the moon-faced boy pressed his palms to the earth and stood up on Koppelberg.

'That music!' he said. 'What music! When the Piper started to play, I heard him promise and promise me: a happy land, right next to the town, where rainbows dance in waterfalls and horses have eagles' wings and nothing is not strange. The pear-trees and plum-trees are always in fruit! The roses never fade! And I promise and promise you: your foot will soon be cured.'

The boy's mouth tightened. His friends! His sharings and secret dreams

13

and games and laughter! High on the hill, he left behind his childhood, and began to make his way back to Hamelin.

GODFATHER DEATH

One spring morning, Hannah gave birth to her seventeenth child.

Soft green leaves shook on the beech tree; greenfinches sang at the little window; the baby lay pink and blue and blissful in its cot. But Hannah wasn't so happy.

'How can I be glad, Stepan?' she said.

Stepan stood by his wife, smiling and sheepish.

'You poor little thing!' cried Hannah. 'How can we possibly feed you?'

'Heigh-ho!' said Stepan.

'How?' cried Hannah. 'When all the others are so hungry.'

'We'll manage,' said Stepan. 'One way or another.'

'You must find a godfather, Stepan,' said Hannah. 'Someone fair, and generous.'

'There's no one left,' said Stepan.

'No one left?'

'Every man in the village is already

godfather to one of our children.'

'But you'll have to find one,' insisted Hannah.

Stepan walked out of the village and into the forest, wondering what to do. 'Ye-yes,' he said slowly. 'I could! He might understand. All right! I'll ask the king.'

*   *   *

That evening, Stepan rapped his staff against the castle gate.

First he had to wait for a long time before one of the wardens came down to find out what he wanted, and then a nasty rottweiler tried to bite his kneecaps.

Poor Stepan! When he told the warden he wanted the king to be godfather to his new baby, the warden simply howled in his face and booted him out.

'So that's the kind of welcome our king gives his subjects,' said Stepan. 'Well! I'll pay him back. One day I'll pay him back.'

Stepan picked up a twig and broke it

16

into pieces. 'Heigh-ho!' he said. 'In this country the rich are rich and the poor are poor. Life is unfair. And what,' he said, 'what am I going to do now about a godfather?'

* * *

As the daylight failed, and everything became blue, Stepan realized there was a man standing at his right shoulder—almost as if he were Stepan's own shadow. He was wearing an ashen cloak and, somehow, his head looked a bit too large for his body.

'Would I do?' said the man. He sounded as though no one had willingly said yes to him in all his life.

'Do?' said Stepan.

'As a godfather?'

Stepan gave a start. 'Who are you?' he said. 'You look so pale—pale as death.'

'I am Death,' said the man.

Then the two of them walked together. They walked and talked and the end of it was that Stepan accepted Death's offer.

'I'll come to the christening,' said Death, smiling and nodding his large head. 'You can count on me.' Then he disappeared into the shadows.

*   *   *

Stepan hurried home and told his wife what had happened. 'After all,' he said, 'you have to admit Death's fair. He doesn't favour the rich and he doesn't favour the poor—no, he takes us all in his good time. You can't say fairer than that.'

'I'm not sure,' said Hannah.

'He'll make a good godfather.'

'But is he ever generous?'

'We'll have to see about that,' said Stepan.

*   *   *

A few weeks later, the baby was christened. Hannah decorated the church with wildflowers, and Death came and held the baby, as he had promised.

Stepan and Hannah didn't even have

enough money to go to the inn afterwards, to buy a drink for the villagers and their pale-faced guest. But the innkeeper, who was godfather to their eldest son, was a generous man: he invited everyone in, and bought drinks for them himself.

After a while, a fiddler struck up a squeaky tune, and many of the villagers began to dance.

Death put a hand on Stepan's shoulder. 'You've been a good friend to me,' he said.

'Cheers!' said Stepan, and he hiccupped.

'You have,' said Death. 'You've trusted me—and invited me here. I don't have so many friends, you know.'

'I suppose not,' said Stepan.

'I'd like to give you a present,' said Death. 'You and my little godson may not have any money but I can make you rich.'

'Rich?'

'We can go into partnership.'

The fiddler fiddled. The villagers clapped and danced. They began to sing. And Death put his mouth to

Stepan's ear.

'. . . so that's what I suggest,' said Death. 'If I'm standing at the foot of the bed, the person will recover. But if I'm standing at the head of the bed, there's nothing you can do about it. That person's mine.'

Stepan raised his tankard to Death and Death raised his tankard to Stepan. 'Do you understand?' he said, and he kept solemnly nodding his large head.

'Cheers!' said Stepan.

*   *   *

The next morning, Stepan nailed a notice to his cottage door. Just three words: DOCTORUS MEDICUS FANTASTICUS

'Nonsense!' said the priest. 'He's never been to school.'

'His head's as thick as a loaf of bread,' said the baker.

'He doesn't know a thing about medicine,' said Hannah. 'I think he's gone mad.'

But when the tailor's little daughter

cried that she had pins and needles all over, as if the elves were shooting at her, her mother was so desperate she carried her to Stepan's cottage, and laid her on a bed.

'I have a herb which may help,' said Stepan.

He chopped the herb, and put it in a few drops of water, and gave it to the tailor's daughter.

At once, unseen to anyone in the cottage but Stepan, Death appeared. He was standing at the foot of the bed.

How Stepan smiled! And when the tailor's daughter had swallowed the medicine, she sat up and smiled too.

*   *   *

Within an hour, everyone in the village knew about the miraculous recovery of the tailor's daughter. And very soon, all the villages for miles around got to hear about Stepan's astonishing powers.

From far and wide, patients came to be cured: an old man with the shakes, and a woman with knots in her stomach; a little boy with devils in his head, who kept tearing at his own face and arms and legs; a girl who had given up wanting to eat.

Stepan welcomed them all to his tiny cottage and gave them all the same herbal medicine. And unseen to anyone but Stepan, Death was always there. Smiling and sometimes nodding, he stood in his ashen cloak at the end of the bed.

After being cured, each patient gratefully brought Stepan a present— two loaves of bread, a basket of eggs, a goose. Before long, Stepan and his family had enough and more than enough to eat; they were no longer poor.

*　　　*　　　*

That summer, the king fell ill. And while apples and cherries grew thick-waisted on the trees, he became thinner and weaker and no one could say what was wrong with him.

The king's criers went riding from village to village, offering a great reward to anyone who could cure the king. And one of them saw the notice on Stepan's door.

'I could cure him,' said Stepan. 'At a price.'

'But he's your king!' said the crier.

'My king once ignored me . . .'

'But he's so ill.'

'And my family was starving.'

'Name your price,' said the crier.

'When I wake up,' said Stepan, 'I want to see bags of gold swinging from my two apple trees. My well must be awash with wine. Yes, and I want a litter, covered with gold cloth, waiting at my gate.'

'Is that all?' said the crier, grimly.

'For the time being,' said Stepan.

*　　　*　　　*

The king's servants worked all night, and when Stepan woke up, he saw they had satisfied his three conditions. So did half the village, and quite a crowd had gathered by the time Stepan was ready to set off for the palace: the priest, the tailor and the baker, the

23

innkeeper . . . not to mention Hannah and her seventeen children.

'Drink the wine!' called Stepan, as he stepped into the golden litter. 'And share out the gold! In this village, one person's sorrow is everyone's sorrow, and one person's fortune everyone's fortune.'

The king's servants carried Stepan through the forest to the king's castle. Then he was led to the king's bedchamber.

'It's Doctor Stepan, your majesty,' whispered one of the courtiers, 'Doctorus Medicus.'

'FANTASTICUS!' said Stepan, smiling.

Then Stepan, and Stepan alone, saw a figure with a pale face and ashen cloak amongst the courtiers. He was standing motionless at the head of the king's bed, and scowling at the king.

'Oh no!' said Stepan. 'Not you!'

'What is it?' whispered the courtiers.

'Not now of all times!' growled Stepan, staring straight at Death.

'What is it, Doctor Stepan? What is it?'

'Never mind!' said Stepan fiercely. 'Never mind!' Then he narrowed his eyes. 'I have a herb here which may help,' he said. 'But even before that, I want you to turn round the king's bed.'

All the courtiers frowned. The king's pharmacist and herbalist looked at each other. They raised their eyebrows and shook their heads.

'Come on!' said Stepan.

As soon as his bed had been turned round, the king flapped a weedy, spotted hand and struggled to sit up. 'Yes,' he said. 'Much better! Much better!'

'Doctor Stepan,' cried the courtiers.

But then Death slowly walked from the foot of the bed to the head of the bed. The king put his hand over his eyes and fell sideways.

'Again!' cried Stepan. 'Turn it round again!'

For a second time, the courtiers put their padded shoulders to the king's bed and turned it round. For a second time, the king sat up. 'Yes,' he said. 'Very much better!'

'Doctor Stepan! Doctor Stepan!'

25

cried the courtiers.

This time, Death did not move. He looked grimly at Stepan. 'I'll see you very soon,' he said, or seemed to say. And with that, he disappeared.

'Long live the king!' cried the courtiers. 'And long live Doctor Stepan.'

*   *   *

On his way home that evening, Stepan walked into a storm. The whistling wind pinned back his ears, and tossed leaves and twigs and even birds around the sky. Then the rain worked its way through Stepan's clothes and he took shelter in the mouth of a cave.

'That's that!' he said. 'I'll have to sleep in this cave.'

When he entered the cave, Stepan was astonished to see that it was bright with burning candles. On rock tables and ledges, and all over the cavern floor, there were thousands and thousands of lights, some quietly shining, some blue and quivering, some winking.

'Aha!' said a voice.

Then Stepan saw a pale face at the end of the cavern.

'Welcome to my kingdom!' said Death, smiling and making his way towards Stepan.

'Your kingdom?' said Stepan, hesitantly.

'It certainly is,' said Death. 'Each of these candles is one life. Look! Some have only just been lit. Some have a long way to go. But you see this one?'

Stepan stared at a candle that had burned right down to its wick: just a ghost of flame over a molten pool of wax.

'That's the king,' said Death. 'I'll be collecting him late tonight.'

'The king?' said Stepan.

'When the flame goes out,' said Death, 'I go and fetch the body: the corpse belongs to me.'

'But . . .'

'There's nothing you can do about it,' said Death. 'First you live in your world, and then in mine. That's how it is.'

Stepan sucked his cheeks. 'Which is

27

my candle?' he asked.

Death didn't reply.

'Which one is mine?'

'Do you really want to know?' asked Death.

Stepan nodded.

Death pointed to a miserable little stub. It was burning brightly but only had a very little way to go.

'No!' cried Stepan. 'Surely you can do something about it, can't you? We're partners, aren't we? And you're godfather to . . .' Then Stepan had an idea. He narrowed his eyes. 'Look!' he exclaimed. 'Up there!'

While Death raised his large head and peered up at the cavern roof Stepan grabbed a long candle and jammed it down over his own miserable stub.

Then Death looked at Stepan. He saw Stepan's shining eyes and knew what he had done.

'Pick up that candle!' said Death.

Stepan shook his head.

'Pick it up!' growled Death.

So Stepan lifted the long candle.

'You see what you've done?' said

Death. 'You stupid man! You've snuffed out your own life.'

Stepan scratched his head and sighed.

'That comes of trying to trick me for a third time,' said Death. 'You stupid man! You could certainly have had a few days longer.'

'Heigh-ho!' said Stepan. Then he grinned and, stepping forward, he put an arm round Death's shoulders. 'A few days more,' he said, 'a few days less. What's a few days between friends?'

So Death opened his ashen cloak, and drew it gently around Stepan.

*   *   *

One spring morning, when soft green leaves shook on the beech tree, Hannah gave birth to her eighteenth child. He lay pink and blue and blissful in his cot. Hannah wept and called him Stepan.

REETA AND THE COW THAT RAN DRY

Reeta wasn't sure quite how it happened. One moment she was sucking a stripped willow twig, as she walked ahead of her two bony cows along the bottom of the little valley, and the next she had tripped and tumbled and was falling down the earth-hole.

As she fell, Reeta remembered her grandmother's warnings about the underground people.

'Avoid them, Reeta. You never know where you are with them.' And again: 'If you meet them, Reeta, you mind your manners, and whatever you do, never accept food from them.'

'Why not?' Reeta had asked.

'I'll tell you why not. If you eat so much as a mouthful, you'll fall under their spell. You'll vanish from this time and place.'

When Reeta opened her eyes, she saw she was in an earth-house very much the same as her own home, except that it was better furnished, and better lit, and very much larger.

At least twenty of the underground people were sitting and eating by the light of many candles at two long pine tables, and most of them were wearing something red—a red jerkin, a red apron, a pair of red trousers.

'Welcome! Welcome!' they called, getting to their feet. Then Reeta realised she was almost twice as tall as they were—as if, by falling down the earth-hole, she had mysteriously doubled in size.

'You're just in time, Reeta,' said a stout old earth-woman.

'How do you know my name?' asked Reeta.

'There's little enough we don't know about you,' said the old woman. 'We're almost neighbours, aren't we? Anyhow,' she said, sitting Reeta at a table, 'You're just in time. Here's the bread.'

'I'm not hungry,' said Reeta very quickly. 'Thank you.'

'Please yourself!' said the old

woman.

Reeta stared around her: the cheerful rosy faces; the branched candlesticks; and all the different kinds of food—steamed fish, hunks of meat, bowls of porridge with dabs of butter in the middle of them.

'We always eat by candlelight,' said the old woman.

'We can only afford candles once a year,' said Reeta. 'At Christmas.'

A pretty girl of thirteen or fourteen—just a little older than Reeta—jumped to her feet. 'You came out this morning with nothing but a piece of dark bread,' she said. 'Wasn't there anything better you could bring?'

Reeta lowered her eyes.

'You can trust me,' said the earth-girl. 'Look! I'll cut you some fresh bread.'

Reeta stared at the warm, soft loaf, fragrant and fresh from the oven. But hungry as she was, she remembered her grandmother's warning. 'I'm not hungry,' she said.

'We know how poor you are,' said the stout old woman, and many of the underground people clucked and tut-tutted. 'We'd like to help you, Reeta. Sit down and eat a proper meal with us, and we'll give you one of our white cows. You know about our cows?'

Reeta lowered her head. She said nothing and felt miserable.

'All right, Reeta!' said the earth-woman briskly. 'I can see you know what's what. So now we'll really give you a cow.'

'You will?' said Reeta.

'If you do exactly as I say,' said the woman.

'Tell me,' said Reeta.

'As soon as you see her, throw your shawl over her back. Otherwise, she'll never follow you.'

'My shawl,' said Reeta.

'She'll yield twice as much milk as one of yours,' the earth-woman said. 'But only milk her once a day! Never milk her to the last drop! If she runs dry,' said the woman, 'we'll be angry, and you'll know about it.'

Reeta smiled. A cow! A white cow!

'Off you go, then!' said the old earth-woman. 'Since you won't eat anything.'

33

Reeta wasn't sure quite how it happened. One moment the old woman was leading her to the earth-shaft and the next she was rising, rising to the light.

Reeta blinked. There, grazing next to her two bony cows, was a comfortable, pink-eyed, milk-white cow, her udders already low and heavy with milk.

Reeta pulled off her shawl and threw it over the cow's back. Around her, wildflowers winked; birch leaves gossiped; the birds of the forest sang. Reeta walked through the green glades at the bottom of the little valley, and led her cows home.

So that evening, Reeta milked three cows—and her little brother Thomas tried to help her. The white cow yielded as much milk as both the bony cows. Not only that! Reeta saw she still had plenty of milk left over.

Her mother skimmed off the oily cream. She tipped it into the churn and set about making butter. She made junkets and cheese. And before they went to bed that night, everyone in the family sat down in the parlour and drank a long draught of warm bubbly milk.

'God bless the hidden people!' said Reeta's mother.

'Bless the day Reeta was so busy sucking a willow twig,' said her father, 'that she stumbled over an earth-hole.'

And Anna, Reeta's baby sister, blew milk-bubbles.

Very early one morning, Reeta looked at her plump white cow and had an idea. 'Why don't I milk her now,' she said to herself, 'and milk her again when we get back this evening? There can't be any harm in it,' she said. 'No! We'll have milk to spare, and we can sell it. Every day we'll sell some, and then we'll be able to buy . . . oh! combs, lace, dresses. For my father a violin! Something for grandmother—something sweet! A fingle-fangle for Anna! And I'll give two pennies to Thomas.'

As she milked the white cow, Reeta closed her eyes. 'An ox,' she breathed. 'One day I'll buy an ox.' And she saw herself riding on the ox, and they were both garlanded with wildflowers, like the wonderful silk flowers on her mother's wedding dress.

Reeta was so wrapped up in her dreams that she didn't realise she had milked the cow dry. She was still squeezing, squeezing the udders, and when she opened her eyes, she saw the teats were red-raw and bleeding.

'Angry! We'll be angry.' Reeta could see the old woman's scowling face and hear her words. There was no escaping them. 'We'll be angry, and you'll know about it.'

Reeta overturned the milking-stool and hurried from the byre into the kitchen. She called for her mother and father. But when they came stumbling out of their sleep, and went into the byre with their daughter, the white cow was not there. It was as if they had all imagined her. As if she were made of air, and had never been.

*　　　*　　　*

It was a long while before Reeta went back with her two bony cows to the secret green glades at the bottom of the valley, where wildflowers blinked and birds of the forest sang.

She was too afraid of meeting one of the underground people, especially the old earth-woman. She was afraid of her fury.

'I've been waiting for you, Reeta. You're greedy! You're selfish! Unfeeling! How could you?'

But time passed, years passed, and the poor cow-girl began to hope she would meet the underground people for a second time. Perhaps she wanted to explain. Perhaps she wanted to tell them what time had taught her.

The underground people did not care. And they didn't give Reeta a second chance. She looked and looked for her almost-neighbours, but she never saw them again.

THE LADY OF STAVOREN

'The most valuable treasure in the world,' said the Lady of Stavoren.

'But, Lady . . .'

'You heard me! Sail north and east, sail south and west, and bring me the most valuable treasure in the world.'

'Lady!' said the captain again. 'Your husband . . .'

'My husband is dead. His boats are my boats. They're mine, all three of them. And you're in my pay.'

'His contacts and customers,' said the captain. 'Coal and malt. And coloured cloth, and squirrel skins, walrus tusks, amber. All your wealth depends on them.'

'My other boats can carry them, can't they?' said the Lady of Stavoren, and her eyes were flint-grey as the wastes of ocean.

Her captain stood in front of her, sound and stocky, like a beer barrel.

'I don't care how long you're away,' said the Lady of Stavoren.

So the captain and his company made ready for their journey.

They stitched their sails; they strutted around the deck, and stretched and sniffed the air; they laid in stores—bread and ale, salted meat, beans, fruit, honey; they strolled around the little harbour and stopped to talk about nothing in particular with whomsoever they met: the maltster and the salt-merchant, the sailmaker, the old shipwright with hands as big as spades, and the fisherman who had lost his sight in a lightning storm.

Then the tide turned. A little wind sprang up from the north-west, and the seagulls screamed, eager and angry.

The captain and his company took leave of their families. And half the boys in Stavoren jumbled and tumbled about on the jetty, all of them with one and the same ambition: to grow up and go to sea.

The captain and his two mates hoisted the mainsail as the boat left the harbour; it looked like a raised hand, oatmeal and beige and buff.

'Where are we going?' asked the

ship's boy.

'Anywhere,' the first mate said.

'And everywhere,' said the second mate.

'The most valuable treasure in the world,' the captain said to himself. And that night he threw back his head and looked at the silver stars and golden moon for so long his head began to spin.

When the ship called at Iceland, the captain wondered whether to buy whale oil: sufficient oil to keep candles burning in every home in Stavoren on every night for the next twenty years.

When the ship called at Bordeaux, in France, the captain wondered whether to buy wines: wines that made you catch your breath as you nosed them, wines that tasted of a mysterious mixture of velvet and blackberry and energy and oak.

At Goa, in India, the captain wondered whether to buy spices: aniseed and cinnamon, pepper, cumin, cardomon.

In the West Indies, the captain wondered whether to buy a hundred laughing parrots; and when the ship called at London, in England, he wondered whether to buy books—epic poems, love stories, the echoing words of wise men grown old and gone to ground.

'Light,' thought the captain. 'Luxury. Laughter. Learning. Love. Which is the most valuable?' And then he thought, 'Life itself must be more valuable than all of these.' The captain frowned. 'If we return to Stavoren without any cargo, and tell the Lady our lives are the greatest treasures in the world, she'll string us up. She'll leave us out for the wolves.'

So when the ship called at Danzig, the captain bought the finest wheat he had ever seen inside a warehouse: plump grain, firm grain, a satin mountain—pure gold.

'We can live without spices and live without wine,' said the captain. 'But we can scarcely live without wheat, can we?'

'No, cap'n,' said the first mate.

'And you've never seen wheat to compare with this.'

'Never,' said the second mate.

'There you are, then,' said the captain.

'Where?' said the ship's boy.

*   *   *

'Wheat, Lady,' said the captain.

And all the people of Stavoren who had gathered on the jetty to welcome the boat back, grinned and nodded.

'Wheat?' croaked the Lady of Stavoren.

Little grey waves were skipping all over the harbour; halyards were clipping and clapping against masts; and the captain's pale blue eyes were dancing.

'What!' said the Lady. 'Have you gone quite mad?'

'Lady . . .'

'Throw it out!'

'We can scarcely live without wheat,' said the captain. 'Next to our own lives . . .'

'Throw it out!'

'I couldn't do that, Lady.'

'Which side did you load it from?'

'Port,' said the captain.

'All right! In one side and out on the other. Throw it out to starboard.'

The captain and his mates turned away. They lowered the gunwale and the precious cargo slipped and rushed and hissed and sighed and slid into the harbour.

'You'll pay for this!' the blind fisherman called out, waving his stick. 'This terrible waste.'

The Lady pointed at the captain. 'Now get off my boat!' she cried. 'And never come near it again!'

'This terrible waste!' repeated the fisherman. 'When all around you people beg: beg for fish-heads; beg for crusts. One day you'll have to beg yourself.'

'Me!' said the Lady of Stavoren. 'Me? Beg?' She stepped angrily towards the blind man and kicked at his stick. Then she ripped off the beautiful gold ring from the middle finger of her left hand. 'I won't have to beg,' she cried. 'I'll never have to beg for so much as a handful of flour—not until the sea gives me back my ring.'

With that, the Lady of Stavoren hurled the flashing gold ring as far as she could. She hurled it into the harbour and at once it sank fathoms deep.

*   *   *

That was not a happy year for the people of Stavoren. In October, the snarling north-west wind drove one spring tide into the harbour and pegged it there until a second tide piled in on top of it. The dark water smashed its fists through dykes, it slopped and sluiced through maltings and granaries and the salthouse and the sailmaker's barn, it flooded one quarter of the little town.

But still the stormy Zuider Zee offered its salt harvest to those men brave enough to net it: a crop of fish, gaping and squirming, filmed with pearl and opal and silver.

One November day so grey the clouds looked six miles deep, a fisherman caught the most enormous haddock.

'Take it up to the Lady of Stavoren,' he told his little daughter. 'Tell her it's the best fish I've ever caught. Tell her . . . she and only she can afford to buy it.'

The Lady of Stavoren took the bait. She paid the fisherman's daughter well for the flapping haddock, and the haddock grimaced at the Lady as if it had never seen anything so horrible in its entire life.

Then the Lady gave the fish to her cook to stun and gut and steam for her lunch.

'St Peter preserve us!' cried the cook. 'Lady! Look!'

The Lady of Stavoren looked, and there, in the stomach of the fish, lay her gold ring.

Then the November wind put its shoulder to her house and pushed, and the old house creaked and groaned; wintry rain spat at her little leaded panes.

*   *   *

On a fine day at the end of November,

all three of the Lady of Stavoren's ships sailed through the Zuider Zee, stuffed with coal and malt, coloured cloth, squirrel skins, walrus tusks, amber.

But at the harbour mouth, first one ship and then the other two shuddered and slewed round. They foundered and sank. It was as if the sea—or rather, the land beneath the sea—had risen up and stopped them.

And that is exactly what it had done. The three ships had run aground on a new bank, a golden bank under the water.

Before long, a forest of waving cornstalks appeared in the mouth of the harbour. A salt-acre of wheat, quite barren. Ten thousand ears and not a single grain between them.

Mud and grit and sand collected round the corn-stalks. And in time a sandbank broke the surface of the swaying water: the fishermen called it Lady's Sand. The sandbank grew and grew. The harbour of Stavoren became so silted up it was impossible for merchant ships to use it any longer.

The only boats that could sidle down the creeks, and skate over the sandbanks, were a few little fishing-smacks.

Many sea-people left Stavoren. What was there to stay for? They had spent their lives as shipwrights, sail-makers, netmakers, coal-merchants, coopers, maltsters, and now there was nothing for them to do.

They went to Molkwerum. They went to Hindelopen. They made their way along the coast of Friesland in search of new work.

Only a few fishermen and their families stayed—they and the Lady of Stavoren.

The sea-farmers were poor enough but the Lady was even poorer. Her servants had left her; her empty old house peeled and echoed and ached; her boats had gone to the bottom.

Sometimes people saw her wade out to the wheatfield blocking the harbour mouth. They saw her stooping to the ears in case a few had grains in them.

And sometimes the Lady shadowed up to their doors. She came, carrying a bowl, and saying over and over again: 'Please! I beg you! Please can you spare me a handful of flour?'

THOR GOES VISITING

It was almost dark and, in the forest, Thor and his three companions kept stumbling over fallen branches and the roots of trees.

'You must wish you'd stayed at home, Thor,' said the trickster Loki. His eyes gleamed orange-and-green in the half-light.

'Wish?' boomed Thor. 'I wish we'd reached the giants' Great Hall.'

In the gloom, the two gods and their servants, Thialfi and Roskva, came upon a sopping glade and a strange building. So far as they could see, one end was completely open; the entrance was as high and wide as the building itself.

'Anyone at home?' shouted Thor.

'It's better than nothing,' said Loki. 'It will keep the rain off our backs.'

Inside was even stranger. The floor and the walls were quite soft and springy. There was no furniture at all. Still, the four of them were so tired they could have slept anywhere.

At midnight, though, they were woken by a terrible growling; the building began to shake. Then there was a fearsome snort. Then silence again.

'There's some sort of monster outside,' growled Thor. 'You go further in. I'll stand guard.'

Loki and Thialfi and his sister groped their way down the hall, and took shelter in a kind of side-room. But they didn't get much sleep. It was stifling in there. And several times they were woken by a muffled roaring.

As soon as it grew light, Thor put his nose out of doors, and at once he saw the cause of all the noise. A huge giant was lying asleep in the glade, and he was snoring . . .

Thor looked at him grimly. He buckled on the belt that doubled his strength. But the giant woke up and leaped to his feet; he was tall as a pine-tree.

'Ha!' he shouted. 'It's Thor, isn't it? Thunder-god!'

'Who are you?' said Thor.

'Skrymir,' said the giant. 'Big Bloke.'

'That's true,' said Thor.

'Who said you could sleep in my glove?'

'Your glove?' said Thor. And turning round, he saw at once that the strange building with an open end was a giant glove. The side-room Loki and the servants had slept in was the thumb.

The giant seemed friendly enough, so Thor told him they were going to the hall of the giant-king, and asked him to show them the way.

'Why not!' boomed Skrymir. 'I'm heading that way myself. I'll carry your bags for you.'

Skrymir simply dropped Thor's bag and the bags of his companions into his own huge sack. He tied the thongs and slung the sack over his back.

Thor and Loki and Roskva were soon left behind. Even Thialfi, the fastest runner on earth, was hard put to keep up with the giant. But the travellers could always tell which way to go by stopping to listen to the crashing sounds ahead of them.

At dusk, Thor and his friends caught

up with Skrymir. He was sitting under an oak tree.

'I'm dead-beat,' boomed the giant.

'We're starving,' said Thor.

'I can't be bothered with food,' said Skrymir. 'Help yourselves! It's in my sack.' Then Big Bloke rolled over and began to snore again.

But the giant had fastened the sack so cleverly that Thor couldn't loosen the thongs. He struggled and he sweated, but he couldn't get at the food.

'Is this your idea of a joke?' growled Thor. 'All right! Try one of mine!'

Then Thor raised his fearsome hammer, and smashed Skrymir's skull with it.

To Thor's amazement, the giant sat up. 'What was that?' he said. 'Did a leaf fall on my head?' And he went back to sleep.

Thor stood over Skrymir and slammed down his hammer on his forehead for a second time; and again the giant sat up unharmed.

'Now what was that?' he said. 'Did you see an acorn fall on my head?'

Then he went back to sleep.

For a third time Thor struck Skrymir with his hammer. He buried it in the giant's brains—it sank right in, up to the handle. And once more, Skrymir sat up, unharmed.

'Are there any birds up there?' he said. 'I could have sworn some droppings fell on me.'

Next morning, Skrymir led Thor and his starving companions to a hilltop. 'I'd go straight home, if I were you,' he said. 'But if you must go to the Great Hall, you'll find it at the end of that valley. Take my advice! Keep your mouths shut! The giants down there won't stand for any bragging from small fry like you!'

With that, the giant turned his back on Thor, and stumped off towards the mountains.

Thor and his companions walked down to the giant-king's castle. It was enormous. Even the dandelions in the forecourt were twice as tall as men, and the locked gates were so vast that the travellers simply stepped through them, between the bars.

The door of the Great Hall was open, so Thor walked in. Loki stood close behind him, and Thialfi and Roskva who were, after all, only human, stood behind Loki.

'Greetings!' called Thor.

None of the giants took the least notice of him.

'Greetings!' Thor shouted.

'Who are you?' said the giant-king.

'Who do you think?' demanded Thor.

'I would have said Thor,' said the giant-king. 'Thor the Charioteer! But surely he's bigger and stronger . . . not a little runt like you!'

Thor's hand moved to his hammer.

'At any rate,' the giant-king said, 'you can't stay here—not unless you're the master of some skill. And your friends: what can they do?'

'I can eat,' said Loki, and his eyes were flashing. 'No one here can eat as fast as I can.'

'Is that so?' said the giant-king. And while his servants piled a trestle-table with sausages and hunks of meat, he beckoned to a giant at the far end of the hall. 'Here, Logi!' he bawled. 'Come and eat against Loki!'

Loki was given a chair at one end of the table, Logi at the other, and they both began to eat.

They chewed, they mashed, they gobbled, they swallowed, and they met in the middle of the table. Loki had eaten every scrap of meat; he had only left the bones. But Logi had not only eaten the meat; he had eaten the bones and the table as well.

'I would say,' pronounced the giant-king, 'that Loki is the loser.'

And all the giants in the hall gave a scornful shout.

'I can run,' said Thialfi. 'No one on middle-earth can run as fast as I can.'

'Is that so?' said the giant-king. 'You must be a good athlete.'

Then they all walked out of the hall to a level of grass that made a good running-track.

'You, Hugi,' the giant-king told a young giant. 'You're the one to run against this boy.' At a word from the giant-king, Thialfi and Hugi began to run. They skimmed over the ground.

But by the time Thialfi had reached the finishing line, he was a long way behind Hugi. The giant had plenty of time to turn round and welcome him.

'You can certainly run fast, Thialfi,' said the giant-king. 'Very fast. But not fast enough.'

And all the giants shouted for a second time.

'I have no great skills,' said Roskva, as they all trooped back into the hall.

'At least you're honest,' said the giant-king. 'That's better than being a braggart, isn't it, Thor?'

'I can drink,' said Thor, 'and I very much doubt whether anyone here can sink as much as I can.'

'Is that so?' said the giant-king. He beckoned, and a servant brought in a brimming drinking-horn. 'Anyone who can drain this in one draught we call a good drinker. Some people take two. No one here is so feeble he can't finish it off in three.'

Thor was very thirsty—the giant-king hadn't offered him and his companions so much as a drop since they arrived in the hall. He lifted the horn, and with huge slurps he gulped the liquid down.

But when he looked into the horn, Thor was startled to see the level of the drink was only an inch or two lower than before.

'Nothing like enough!' said the giant-king, shaking his head and smiling.

Thor raised the horn to his mouth again and poured a tide of drink down his throat. But he ran out of breath before the horn ran out of liquid. Indeed, when he peered into it, he saw he had made rather less headway than with his first draught.

Thor's red beard bristled. He grabbed the horn and this time he nearly burst with the effort. His head pounded; the hall swam before his eyes. He drank as much as he could stomach, and there was a strange salty taste in his mouth. But he was still unable to empty the horn.

'Oh dear!' said the giant-king. 'You're not much of a drinker, are you, Thor! Do you want to try your hand at something else?'

'What?' said Thor, gruffly.

'How would you like to wrestle? You see my grey cat? Young giants here like to lift him off the ground.'

The giant-king's grey cat uncoiled and sprang across the floor. He was as tall as Thor himself, and every time Thor gave a heave, the cat simply arched his back.

Now Thor stood right under the cat. And when he stretched his hands and the cat's belly as high above his head as he could, the cat had to lift one paw off the ground.

'Much as I thought!' boomed the giant-king. 'I suppose he is rather a big cat for a midget like you.'

'I haven't come here to play with cats,' shouted Thor. 'Let's have some proper wrestling.'

The giant-king looked around the hall. 'I can't say I see anyone here . . .' he said. 'They'd all think it was beneath them. I've an idea! My old foster-mother, Elli!'

An ancient woman came hobbling across the hall. White-haired. Black-toothed. Her back was almost bent double.

When Elli saw Thor, she grinned and threw away her stick.

Then Thor fairly hurled himself at her, but the moment he laid hold of her, he knew he was in for a fight. The old woman was strong, immensely strong. Thor heaved, he strained and grunted, but she didn't flinch.

Then Elli got the upper hand. She put an armlock on Thor and, with a wrist as strong as iron, began to force him downward. Thor lost his balance; he clung to Elli desperately; the veins stood out on his forehead. But it was no use. The god dropped on to one knee.

All the giants in the hall shouted and banged the trestle-tables with their fists.

'Enough!' shouted the giant-king. 'Enough, Thor! You've shown us all how strong you are.'

Then the giants made room for Thor and his friends at the crowded benches. The travellers ate and drank as much as they wanted, and that night they slept beside the fire in the Great Hall.

Early next morning, Thor and his

companions were eager to set off for home, and the giant-king escorted them.

'You've put me to shame,' said Thor. 'I've come off second best, I can't deny it.'

'Listen, Thor!' said the giant-king. 'Now we're safely out of my castle, I'll tell you the truth. I've been using spells to trick you.'

Loki began to grin a twisted grin.

'You remember Skrymir?'

'In the forest,' said Thor.

'I'm Skrymir.'

'You?' said Thor.

'I changed my appearance so you couldn't recognise me,' said the giant-king. 'Yes, and I fastened my sack with wires so you couldn't open it. And you see that hill over there with those three huge craters? I put it between us when you tried to hit me. You made those craters with your hammer.'

The Thunder-god scowled.

'And down here in the hall! When Loki ate all that meat, he was competing against Logi—and Logi is Wildfire itself. He burned up the table as well as the meat. And when Thialfi ran against Hugi, he was running against my own Thought. No one can keep up with the speed of Thought.

'And you, Thor,' said the giant-king. 'That horn: you didn't realise the other end was in the sea. No wonder you couldn't empty it! When you get home, have a look at how much the tide has ebbed. You've stranded half the ships in the German Ocean.

'As for the cat! It's the gigantic Midgard serpent which encircles the whole earth. You grazed its back against the sky. Everyone was amazed when you made it lift one paw.

'And Thor! How did you withstand Elli for so long? Elli is Old Age. No one can resist her. Sooner or later, she brings everyone to their knees.'

Thor was seething. He began to finger the handle of his hammer, Mjollnir.

'It will be better for us both if you never come near my Great Hall again,' said the giant-king. 'And now you're angry, so before you can use that hammer of yours, I'll make one last spell.'

Thor raised Mjollnir over his head. He summoned all his strength.

But the giant-king had vanished. So had the castle, and the lounging giants, and the Great Hall. It was just as if Thor and his companions had dreamed everything, except that there in front of them stood the hill with the three craters.

Thor rubbed his eyes and shook his head; Loki arched his eyebrows.

'East, west,' said Thialfi, putting a hand on Thor's right arm.

'Home is best,' said his sister, Roskva.

THE UGLY DUCKLING

How lovely it was in the summer country. Green oats, and wheat green-and-gold; the thick, sweet smell of newly-scythed hay.

The storks went walking through the shining fields on their long red legs, walking and talking Egyptian, just as they had been taught to do by their mothers. There were woods surrounding the fields, and in the woods dozens of little lakes and pools.

The sunlight settled on the shoulders of the ancient castle. It winked in the moat. It warmed all the outstretched hands of the burdocks that grew so thick and tall you could walk under them and pretend you were in the middle of the forest.

And amongst these burdocks, between the castle and the moat, a duck had built her nest.

One by one her eggs cracked; one by one, little heads poked out, little eyes blinked, little beaks opened. 'Peep!'

they said. 'Peep!'

'Quack!' said their mother. 'Look around you!'

So the ducklings blinked at the green world, and the green was good for their eyesight.

'How large the world is!' peeped the baby ducklings.

'Large!' said their mother. 'You haven't seen half of it. It stretches as far as the priest's cornfield.' When the duck stood up, she saw one of her eggs—the biggest one—had still not hatched. 'Bother!' she said. 'How much longer? I'd like to go for a swim.'

Then one of the old ducks came flouncing through the burdock to visit her.

'Look at them!' said the mother duck. 'Aren't they the sweetest things you ever saw? They all look just like their father.'

'That scoundrel!' said the old duck.

'But one egg won't hatch.'

'Let me have a look at it,' said the old duck. 'Yes, that's a turkey's egg. You don't want to bother with that. Turkey chicks won't even go near the water.'

'I'll sit on it just a little longer,' said the duck.

'It's up to you!' said the old duck, and she flounced off through the burdock.

At last the big egg cracked open and the chick fell out. 'Peep! Peep!' he said. He was very large and very ugly.

'He's so large, and doesn't look like the others at all,' said the mother duck. 'I wonder if he really is a baby turkey.'

But next day, when the mother duck took her babies down to the moat, she didn't have to nip or kick the ugly duckling to get him into the water.

'He's not a turkey,' the mother duck said. 'He knows what to do with his legs. He holds his neck up straight. He's my own baby. In fact,' she said, 'if you look at him carefully, he's rather handsome.'

Later that day, the duck led her family to the henyard to meet everyone.

'Keep close to me,' she said, 'and then no one will step on you. And watch out for the cat!'

In the henyard, two families of ducks were pecking and squabbling over an eel's head. But neither of them got it! The cat pounced on it.

'That's how life is,' the mother duck told her ducklings. 'Quack! Don't walk! Waddle properly—keep your legs well apart, like I do. And now,' she said, 'come and bow to the old duck over there. She has Spanish blood. She's a lady or a countess or a duchess. That's why she's so fat. And you see that red rag tied round her leg? It's a great honour. It means the farmer will never kill her.'

Other ducks began to gather round the mother duck and her little family.

'We don't want this bunch, do we?'

'There's enough of us here already.'

'Look at the ugly one! We're not having him.'

Then one duck actually bit the ugly duckling on the neck.

'Leave him alone!' the mother duck shouted. 'He hasn't harmed you.'

'He's too big,' said the biter-duck. 'He's not like anyone else. Isn't that good enough reason?'

66

'What lovely little children!' said the old duck with the red rag around her leg. 'All except one.'

'He's ever so obliging, my lady,' said the mother duck. 'And he can swim just as well as the others. In fact, even a little better. It's just that he was in the egg too long . . . He'll grow more handsome . . . Anyhow, he's a drake, so his looks don't really matter.'

'Well, the other ones are pretty,' the old duck said. 'Make yourselves comfortable.'

But the poor little duckling was jostled and bitten by the other ducks and even by the hens. The turkey cock strutted up and gobbled at him until he was red in the face. The sad little creature wished he were not so ugly, and didn't know where to hide.

And this was just the first day; after this, every day was worse than the one before. The poor duckling was even chased around by his own brothers and sisters, and they kept quacking, 'You ugly creature! If only the cat would get you!'

The ducks bit him. The hens pecked

him. The hen-girl kicked him. And finally even his mother said, 'I wish you weren't here—I wish you were a long way away.'

Then the duckling ran away. He flew a long way away until he reached a great marsh where wild ducks lived, and he was so tired he stayed there for the night.

Next morning, the wild ducks discovered him.

'What sort of bird are you?' asked one.

'You're certainly ugly,' said another. 'But that doesn't matter, so long as you're not thinking of marrying one of my daughters.'

The ugly duckling spent two days in the marsh, swimming amongst the reeds, sipping water. Then two wild geese—two young ganders—flew up to him.

'Listen, mate!' they said. 'You're so ugly we really rather like you. Do you want to come with us? Some pretty young geese live near here and you could try your luck with them. Come on!'

'Bang! Bang!'

The two young ganders fell into the reeds, dead; the water turned red around them.

'Bang! Bang!' the whole marsh was surrounded by guns. Guns in the bushes; guns amongst the reeds; guns in the trees. A great skein of wild geese started up. There was blue smoke over the marsh, and the sound of splashing dogs.

The poor little duckling was terrified. Just as he was tucking his head under his wing, so as to hide himself, he saw a large dog eyeing him through the reeds. The dog's tongue was hanging out and it bared its teeth. But then splash!—splash! It just turned away.

'Mercy!' cheeped the little duckling. 'I'm so ugly not even the dog wants me.'

The shooting went on until the middle of the afternoon. And it was several hours after that before the frightened little duckling dared raise his head from under his wing. Then he ran away. He scooted out of the marsh, and across the fields, fighting his way into the wind.

At dusk, the ugly duckling spied a little hut so crooked that there was only one reason why it was still standing up: it couldn't decide which way to fall over. An old woman lived in it with her cat, who could arch his back and purr, and make sparks if you stroked his fur in the wrong direction, and her hen, who laid lots of eggs. The old woman loved her like a daughter.

In the dark, the duckling squeezed into the hut through the crack where the door had come off its hinges, and next morning the cat and hen discovered him.

'Aha!' said the woman (she was rather short-sighted and thought the duckling was already grown-up). 'We're in luck! We'll have duck eggs before long, unless it's a drake.'

The duckling stayed in the hut for three weeks, but of course he laid no eggs. And the cat and the hen, who thought they knew everything, scarcely let the duckling open his mouth.

'Can you lay eggs?' asked the hen.

'No,' said the duckling.

'Shut up, then!'

'Can you arch your back?' asked the cat. 'Do you know how to purr? Or make sparks?'

'No.'

'In that case, what you have to say isn't worth hearing.'

But when the duckling started to think about fresh air and sunlight, he so longed to go swimming he couldn't bear not to talk about it.

'Swimming! What a ridiculous idea!' said the hen. 'The trouble with you is you've nothing to do. If you could lay eggs, or purr, you'd soon forget about swimming.'

'It's so lovely to float on water,' said the duckling, 'and wet your head, and dive to the bottom.'

'So lovely,' said the hen. 'I think you've gone mad. Quite mad! Ask the cat if he likes swimming and diving to the bottom! Ask the old woman if she likes floating on water and getting her hair wet!'

'You don't understand . . .' cried the duckling.

'Don't understand, don't I?' said the hen. 'The cat and I—and the old woman—we all understand a great deal more than you ever will. It's time you did some work. Lay some eggs! Purr! Arch your back!'

'No,' said the duckling. 'I'm going to see the wide world for myself.'

'You do that!' said the hen.

So the duckling left the hut. He walked and he flew until he came to a lake where he could float and dive to the bottom. The other ducks there turned their backs on him because he was so ugly.

Autumn came and the yellow and brown leaves danced in the wind; winter followed and the clouds sagged with snow and hail. 'Ow! Ow!' croaked a raven perched on a fence. 'Ow! Cold!'

One day, as the winter sun set in a flood of fire, a flock of the most beautiful birds floated out of the rushes. Their feathers were shining white; their necks were long and graceful; they were swans. The swans whooped, and beat their strong, stately wings, they climbed and circled, and the ugly duckling spun round and round in the water like a wheel, and reached out for the sky, and cried with longing.

Then the swans flew away south to a warmer country, and the duckling dived to the bottom of the lake. He was so miserable. He knew he loved these birds—loved them far more than he had ever loved anyone before; and he didn't know where they were going. He didn't even know their names.

It grew cold and then even colder. The ice on the lake muttered and groaned and the duckling had to swim round and round to keep his little water hole open. But each night his space became smaller and in the end he was too worn out to swim any longer. The ice closed round him and locked him in.

Next morning, a farmer found the duckling. He kicked away the ice around him, and freed him; he put him under one arm and took him back to his wife.

The duckling was so scared of the

farmer's playful children that he spread his wings and splashed straight into the milk pail—from there, he blundered into the butter churn, and then he flapped into the flour barrel.

The farmer's wife was furious. She shouted at the duckling and chased him with a poker, and the duckling flew out of the farmhouse door. He lay very still under some bushes, in a little drift of snow.

That was a terrible winter for the duckling. But for all that, he managed to survive. Once more the sun shone warmly on his back, little larks climbed and sang; spring had come again.

Then the duckling spread his wings—they were so strong now and stately. He climbed and he flew and, far from the lake, he saw a lovely garden. The apple-trees were in blossom there, and white and purple lilac bent low over a winding canal.

Then out of the reeds floated three swans. They ruffled their feathers; they sat so lightly on the water, and for a second time the duckling was filled with an overwhelming sadness.

'They're royal birds,' he said, 'and I'll fly down to them. They can rip me to pieces because I'm so ugly . . . because I tried to speak to them. Well, I'd rather give my life to them than be bitten by ducks, and pecked by hens, and kicked by the hen-girl, and frozen by the bitter cold.'

So the duckling flew down to the water. He swam towards the royal swans. And the swans turned to meet him.

The poor thing lowered his head and stared into the water, and waited for the swans to peck him and kill him. But what did he see? He saw he was no longer grey and gangling, no longer graceless or awkward or ugly. He was a swan!

The three swans encircled him and gently nuzzled him with their beaks.

Some children came down to the canal with bread for the swans.

'Look! There's a new one!' shouted the youngest, and they all hared back indoors to tell their parents.

Then the whole family fed the swans with bread and cake, and they all agreed the new one was the most lovely of all. The older swans kept bowing to him.

He felt very shy, and he tucked his head under one wing. He was happy, so happy. The white and purple lilac bent right down to the water for him. The sun shone warmly for him. He ruffled his feathers; he arched his slender neck. 'When I was the ugly duckling,' he said, 'I never knew there was happiness such as this.'

THE ARMY OF BEARS

Deep in the forest, the King of Berne came face to face with the bear he had been tracking all day long. He came lolloping through the trees and, of all the bears the young king had hunted, he was the biggest.

The bear looked sadly at the king. He rocked backward as the king jabbed at him with his shining sword; he ducked as the king swiped at him. Then he struck the young man a terrible blow to the side of the head with his left paw, dragging his claws across the king's ear and cheek. The king cried out and fell to the ground.

A forester working nearby heard the cry. He ran through the forest and saw the giant brown bear standing over the young king. Then he raised his axe, and shouted, and split open the bear's skull.

The forester slung the unconscious king over his shoulder, as if he were a lamb, or a limb of wood for the fire, and carried him back to his cottage.

There, his daughter Rowena looked at the young man—his whey-white face, his long dark hair. With spring water she washed his deep wounds. She soaked a piece of muslin with boiled camomile and witchhazel, and gently pressed it to them. For many days she sat beside him, and tended him, and wondered who he was.

One day, the young King of Berne opened his eyes. He saw Rowena smiling, and so beautiful. 'Who are you?' he asked. 'Where am I?'

'And you, who are you?' Rowena asked softly.

For three more days, the king lay in the forester's cottage. And on the third evening, he told the forester, 'You saved my life. I want to take you back to my castle, and honour and reward you. And if Rowena accepts me, I will marry her.'

* * *

During the young king's absence, the King of Burgundy had captured his castle and set fire to half his kingdom.

No sooner did he step out of the forest with Rowena and the forester than a troop of twenty bristling Burgundians rushed out from behind a great rock and swarmed around them.

'God save the king!' cried Rowena.

The king with his sword and the forester with his axe did their utmost to put up a fight, but while the king was shouting encouragement to his companions, three Burgundians ran at him at the same time. They knocked the king over backwards, and then one man fell on him, squeezing his lifebreath out of his body.

When the king came to his senses, he realised he was lying at the foot of a great rock, alone. The forester and Rowena had disappeared, and so had the troop of Burgundians.

The king struggled to his feet. 'Rowena!' he called. 'Rowena!' He shouted for help; he shouted to heaven. But no one heard him and no help came.

Then the king turned his back on Berne and, slowly, he limped away towards the high mountains. Hot tears trickled down his grimy cheeks.

That night, the king slept in a forest glade. His mattress was made of pine needles; his ceiling was punctured with stars; and his sleeping companion was the trunk of an uprooted tree.

At dawn, the king was woken by warm breath on his face. And when he opened his eyes, he saw an enormous dog, almost as big as a bear, looking down at him.

The king scrambled to his feet and the dog bared his teeth and grinned. 'Yes! Yes!' he barked. 'Follow me!'

The dog led the king on towards the mountains. They crossed little plashing streams, they climbed out of the forest into sunlight, and at last they came to the cave of Wilfred the Hermit.

They came to a clearing in the forest and there stood a gigantic bear with black fur.

As soon as the bear-king saw Wilfred, he splayed out his front paws, and bowed right down in front of him.

'So Rab found you,' said the hermit.

The king nodded.

'And you're in trouble,' the hermit

said.

Then the king told Wilfred everything that had happened to him since he had left his castle to go bear-hunting. The hermit said nothing. He just leaned on his stick and looked at the king with his faded, sky-blue eyes.

When the king had finished, the hermit gave a long low-whistle, and at once a crow came flapping into the cave.

'I want you to fly all over the kingdom,' said Wilfred. 'Find out the fate of Rowena and her father.'

The crow winked at the king, and the king saw it had only one eye. Then it flew down from the mountainside, and three days passed before it returned to the cave.

'They're alive!' whistled the crow. 'But stone a crow! Talk about danger!'

'What danger?' asked the king.

'The King of Burgundy has imprisoned them. Rowena's in a high tower, and her father's in chains, lying in a dungeon.'

'Yes! Yes!' barked Rab. 'I know what we can do.'

'What, Rab?' asked the hermit.

'Master, the King of the Bears was once so sick, and you cured him with herbs. You saved his life, Master, and now—with all his strength—he'll help you. Yes! Yes!'

Wilfred was very old, he could only limp along slowly, leaning on his stick, and it was many days before he and the King of Berne, accompanied by Rab and the one-eyed crow, at last reached the village of Orsières, the valley of Great St Bernard, and the Kingdom of the Bears.

'This is the young King of Berne,' said the hermit. 'The King of Burgundy has captured his castle and set fire to half his kingdom, and imprisoned his love. We need your help. We need all your strength.'

'The King of Berne!' growled the huge bear. 'He can think himself lucky I haven't ripped off his head. He and some forester murdered my brother!'

'You are not to speak like this,' said the hermit.

The huge bear rocked to and fro.

'No!' said the hermit. 'Do not be

bitter. Try to render good for evil.'

The bear-king bowed and swayed and his black coat bristled. He growled again, but in his heart he was touched by the hermit's words. 'Your will be done,' he murmured. 'I will help the King of Berne.'

Then the king swore that never again would he hunt a bear. 'I will honour you,' he said, 'and all other bears because of you, as the guardian of my crown.'

The bear-king reached out a large paw, and with both hands the King of Berne grasped it. Then the bear-king hugged him to his hairy chest.

After this, the King of Bears opened his mouth and roared. He roared and prowled round the forest clearing, sometimes pausing to glare through the pine trees.

From all around, other bears began to answer the roars of the bear-king. Then more bears started to answer them—bears much further off, bears as far away as distant memories. So that, before long, mountain-top and glacier, waterfall, forest and valley were all caught up in one continuous roar-and-echo.

All night long, the roaring went on, and at dawn Wilfred and the king saw the whole clearing was packed with brown bears and black bears.

Then one bear unfurled a banner: it was scarlet, with a gold diagonal band; and on the gold band was a black bear with his tongue hanging out.

At a signal from their king, the army of bears all set off down the mountainside, followed by the King of Berne and Wilfred the Hermit, and faithful Rab, and the one-eyed crow. Shambling and swaying and groaning, they trampled over wildflowers in the high mountain pastures; they flattened little plots of white-gold corn; they squashed precious beds of wild strawberries. Everyone who saw them—children, women and men—ran yelling and squealing into their châlets.

That night, the bears slept at the foot of a glacier. Rab and the crow stayed, but Wilfred and the young king slept alongside them. The king had never had such a choice of furs to keep him warm!

As soon as the King of Burgundy saw the army of bears approaching he gave orders that the castle gates should be closed. Huge oak doors were swung shut; the massive portcullis was lowered.

The crow sailed high over the castle walls. He stared down with his one unwinking eye, and reported back to the bear-king: 'The Burgundians are about to rain arrows on to you.'

Then the bear-king ordered his army to attack. First the little bears scooped up stones and hurled them at the Burgundian archers standing on the castle walls. Then the great bear-army charged at the castle from all sides, bounding from ledge to ledge, leaping over the battlements, snarling and launching themselves at the mounted Burgundians inside the castle walls.

The Burgundian horses had never seen such enemies! They snorted and bucked and threw their riders. Then the army of bears fell on their enemies—they clubbed them, they mauled them, and they smothered them.

The King of Burgundy soon saw the battle was lost. One of his buglers sounded the retreat, and the remains of his army streamed out of the castle, and galloped away to the west.

So the bear-king welcomed the young King of Berne back into his own castle. Quickly the king found Rowena in the high tower; he kissed her and freed her. And he found her father in the dungeon and unchained him.

Then Wilfred the Hermit married the young king and Rowena in the castle chapel. Rab sat in one corner, occasionally thumping his tail; the crow perched on a chandelier. Some of the wedding guests sang; some of them hummed; some of them growled!

After this, the wedding-feast began: a banquet for humans and bears, bears and humans. There was ant-pie and skewered cheese and honeycake and wild strawberries; there was mountain water and golden wine.

At dawn, the bear-king lumbered up to the King of Berne. 'Will you give us leave to go now?' he said gruffly. 'You know how far it is to the Kingdom of the Bears.'

'I've one more favour to ask of you,' said the king. 'Will you give me your bear-banner?'

The bear-king bowed and presented the King of Berne with the magnificent banner.

'Let this be the banner of Berne,' cried the young king, 'today and for ever.'

'Amen!' said Wilfred the Hermit, and he waved his stick in the air.

Then all the bears growled very softly—a sound like the sound of hundreds of bees content in a summer field, lit by sunlight.

The King of the Bears turned away. He swayed through the great oak doors and under the portcullis. He and his army lolloped out of the castle, and into memory.

WITH MY RIGHT HAND

The young stranger had been so used to the clap of the waves and the company of kittiwakes. It felt odd to sail into the quiet estuary and up to the fine city; odd to stand on dry ground again.

On the wharf he listened to a fish auction; he chased a pig's bladder and threw it back to a mob of children. But the more people he saw, the more lonely he felt. How he wished he were back in his own country, with his own family. The young man crouched on a mooring-post. He combed his right hand through his fair hair and, for a long time, he stared into the drifting water.

The stranger became light-headed with hunger. He walked across the city to the market-place, and made his way to a fruit-stall. He fished for his last coin, and reached out for a beautiful, rosy apple.

But another hand reached out for

the same apple. It got there first! And when the young man turned round to see whom it belonged to, he found himself looking into the eyes of a lovely, laughing girl.

'Snap!' she said.

'Who are you?' he asked.

'The princess! The princess!' whispered voices all around him.

When the princess saw how exhausted the stranger was, she pressed the apple into the palm of his hand, and closed his fingers round it. Then she took his arm and led him back to the palace.

*   *   *

In the palace, the young man met the king and the princess' two elder sisters, Alga and Hadei. 'I'm on my way home,' he told them. 'I've been away for a year.'

'A year!' exclaimed the princess.

'And how long since you ate a square meal?' enquired the king. 'You stay here! Stay here with us until you're ready to continue your journey. My daughters will look after you.'

In the following days, the blond stranger and the princess explored the city's narrow cobbled streets; they played ball with the princess' terrier; they ran round the whole circuit of the ancient city walls; they sat cross-legged on the young man's boat. And the more time they spent together, the more they grew to love one another.

Alga shook salt into the princess' apple-pie.

Hadei dribbled red sealing wax over the stranger's woollen surcoat.

But they were powerless; the young man only had eyes for the princess.

'When I reached your city,' he told the princess, 'I wanted to hurry home. But now,' he said, 'I scarcely want to go home at all—or not alone.'

One afternoon, late, a carrier pigeon flew into the estuary and up to the fine city. It brought a message to the young stranger from his elder brother:

'Our father must leave on a long journey. Set sail! Come home!'

So the young man thanked the king of the fine city for his kindness. He bowed to Alga and to Hadei. Then he took the princess' hand and led her down to the quay. 'Before long,' he said, 'I will come back for you.'

The stranger hoisted his sail; it flapped like a wild wing. He waved to the princess and his little boat ran before the wind down and out of the estuary. Then the young man veered north, he sailed back to his own country, where his father was the king.

It took the stranger seven days to get home. He greeted his mother and his brother, he clasped and kissed his old father, and that same night his father died with a long sigh and something like a smile.

Then the old man's body, light as a bird, was laid in the bows of a bucking ship; his corpse was covered with blossoms; coloured shields were hung in a row over the ship's railings.

A square black sail was hoisted, and the ship sailed out to sea, the king its only passenger.

The two brothers fired burning arrows at the ship. Away it sailed, cradled in flames. It disappeared far out, far off, somewhere between the waves and the heavens.

Then the elder brother became king of the country.

'No one wins fame by staying at home,' he said. 'No one gets rich by sitting on his backside. Let's sail south. Let's raid fine cities! Rob monasteries!'

The two brothers examined canvas maps, and the young man was alarmed to see that his elder brother was planning to attack the fine city on the banks of the grey river.

He thought of the friendly wharf; the narrow cobbled streets; above all, he thought of the princess.

'Not that city!' said the young man.

'Why not?' demanded the king. 'It's the richest of them all.'

'I was there,' said the young man. 'They were good to me.'

'I'll go where I like,' said his brother. 'And you'll come with me.'

'No!' cried the young man.

'You traitor!' shouted the king.

The two brothers began to argue, and then they drew their swords. At once several of their friends stepped between them, risking their own lives.

'Words are better than blades,' mumbled the dead king's chamberlain, an old man without a tooth in his head. 'I'll tell you what. Race from here to the city! Race to the city walls! If the king touches them first, the city will be plundered and burned to the ground. If his brother gets there first, the city will be left in peace.'

The two brothers accepted the old man's suggestion.

Next morning, they and their followers boarded two warships, shouting and singing. They hoisted their sails; they manned their oars; they went south over sea.

Side by side, the two ships raced towards the fine city. Often the young stranger stood in the bows, with one hand on the dragon prow, staring out across the iron-grey water. The bright mob of children; the terrier, yapping; the race around the old walls; above all, his laughing princess . . .

'Faster!' cried the young man. 'Faster!'

And his oarsmen spat on their

palms, and grunted.

When the city watchmen saw two Viking ships racing up the estuary, they shouted warnings. Hundreds of men armed themselves with spears and shields and climbed up on to the city walls.

Then the great bell began to ring. Women and children crowded into the church, and over and again they prayed, 'From the fury of the Norsemen, from the fury of the Norsemen, good Lord, deliver us.'

The princess sat alone in the tower room of the palace, as she had done since the young stranger had left the city. 'Where is he?' she whispered. 'He said he would come back. I love him so and won't he come to save me? Won't I ever see him again?'

The two Viking ships raced to the city wharf. Their sails billowed; their oarsmen gritted their teeth. The blond stranger and the king stood poised by their prows, still neck-and-neck.

The brothers jumped down on to the wharf. They sprinted away from the dock, they ran through the park and across the market-place, towards the city walls.

The princess' terrier was the first to recognise the young stranger. It ran down from the palace tower, and rushed out to greet him.

But the terrier got under the young man's feet. It tripped him up and the stranger fell sprawling on his face.

So the young king ran ahead of his brother; the walls loomed up in front of him, mossy and tottering. There was no stopping him now.

The stranger drew his knife; its edge was deadly and gleaming. He screwed up his eyes, pulled back his lips, and chopped off his right hand at the wrist.

At once the young man picked up his hand. He hurled it, far and shining. It touched the city walls just as his gasping brother was reaching out for victory.

So the fine city on the banks of the grey river was saved. It was saved and the princess was filled with excitement and pride and love when she realised who had saved it.

On the very next day, there was a

great celebration in the palace, and the princess and the blond stranger were married.

The young man put a broad ring on the princess' left hand. But the princess pressed the stranger's right hand to his wrist—and such was her love that the hand and wrist grew together. They healed. They became one again. The only sign of the young man's courage was, as it were, a red silk thread where they had joined.

Everyone sang, they drank mead, and feasted; and the young king of the north country even danced with the princess' two elder sisters. Alga and Hadei, Hadei and Alga: he couldn't decide which one was worse.

'Such bravery must never be forgotten,' said the princess' father. 'Our fine city on the banks of the grey river: we could call it "hurl-a-hand". Yes, hand werpen! Let us call it Antwerp!'

PERSEPHONE, RISING

Where rock-roses blush and wild tulips shine; where poplars tremble and silver-grey olives claw the ground; where misty mauve grapes swell and sweeten; where ears of wheat and barley ripen: here, too, were gentle Demeter and her daughter Persephone.

The life of each plant and tree was as precious to Demeter as the life of her own daughter, and each prospered only because Demeter watched over them.

How lovely Persephone was! Her cheeks were quite rosy and she had such a look—a daring look—in her tawny eyes. And the rapids of her hair! As brown is golden; as honey; as the force in the barley; so was her hair.

Some people said Persephone's father was Zeus himself, father of the gods, and Demeter's own brother. As she grew up, she attracted a swarm of suitors: mighty gods, and less-than-gods, human men, and more-than men.

Zeus' eldest brother, Hades, asked Persephone more than once to rule over the underworld with him. When she refused, Hades turned for help to Zeus. 'Allow me,' he said, 'to take Persephone down under the earth.'

The father of the gods didn't want to upset his brother and didn't want to anger his sister—he felt as if he were passing between the rock of Scylla and the whirlpool of Charybdis.

So in the end he didn't say yes and didn't say no; he rubbed his beard, and looked at Hades and said nothing.

In the cool of the evening, Persephone and her friends, the river nymphs, went out to pick wildflowers: black-and-red arum lilies, and wild cyclamen.

Then Persephone found the beautiful hundred-blossomed narcissus—some people say Hades' flower. But as she stooped to it, she heard the sky hum and rumble away to the north and saw a dark cloud rushing towards her.

The girls called out to each other; they ran towards the fig trees. But Persephone stood her ground, white and gold; the dark cloud throbbed and hovered over her.

When Persephone looked into the heart of the cloud, she saw Hades there in his ebony chariot, drawn by four charcoal horses. Their eyes were as fiery as blood-red rubies and the eyes of Hades were glittering like two freezing sapphires.

Hades reached out and grabbed Persephone, he dragged her into his chariot, and Persephone screamed.

But at once the horses galloped away. They galloped through pine forests, they galloped over dry mountains, until they reached the river Cyane.

Cyane saw Persephone helpless in the chariot. At once she reared up; she rose up to save her and swamp Hades in one great wave of hyacinth-and-jade-and-indigo.

But Hades drove his terrible two-pronged spear into the river bank. The earth opened. Then the King of the Underworld drove his chariot down into the earth and, as he did so, Persephone cried out again; she tore off her golden girdle, and threw it into the weeping river.

*   *   *

Demeter had heard her daughter's cry when Hades dragged her into his chariot.

The goddess went to the lip of Mount Etna and lit two torches from the flames of the volcano. For nine nights and nine days she hurried through forests and over mountains, searching and calling out for her daughter. She didn't eat; she didn't drink; she didn't wash; and she carried a burning torch in each hand.

Demeter forbade plants and trees to grow. Grapes shrivelled; grass withered; yellow crocuses sighed and fell over sideways. Everything that rises from its earth-prison suffered for Persephone.

On the evening of the ninth day, Demeter found Persephone's golden girdle. It was snagged among the reeds in the river Cyane, close to a little weir.

The seething water spoke to the

goddess: 'I saw Persephone! Hades has stolen her. And my hidden sisters, with their unblinking eyes they have seen her: she was sitting on her skull-throne next to grinning Hades.'

Demeter was so sad she could not even sob. She went away alone to a dry cave, dusty, a place of echoes.

Days passed, weeks passed, on earth nothing grew, and many things died. Poppies bled; anemones closed their violet eyes; olive trees groaned and creaked. The hard earth gleamed—it was almost glassy.

Demeter would not relent. She allowed nothing to grow and people on earth became thirsty and hungry. They began to starve. Then men and women went to Zeus, the sky-god, and begged for his help.

Zeus was troubled. He rubbed his beard, and called for his son, the winged messenger Hermes.

'Tell Hades,' he said, 'that unless he returns Persephone, nothing can grow on earth. Without food, people and animals will die; without prayers, gods will die. Tell him there will be no life and no death.

'And tell my sister,' said Zeus, 'tell Demeter she can bring her daughter back from the underworld on one condition: that Persephone has not eaten the food of the dead. Not so much as a mouthful! Not even a pip!'

As soon as Demeter heard what Zeus had to say, she hurried with Hermes to the grove of black poplars overlooking the sea. And there they went down into the underworld.

Charon the miser ferried them across the river Styx, and three-headed Cerberus knew they were coming—he did not even bark, but allowed them to pass. Then they crossed fields shining with pale petals where thousands of ghosts drifted around them, twittering like bats. They hurried past the three ghastly Furies, with their corpse-black bodies and dogs' heads and snake-hair, their bats' wings and blazing red eyes.

So Demeter and Hermes reached the white cypress and the river of Forgetting, and beyond it the palace belonging to Hades.

And Demeter saw her daughter,

Persephone, sitting golden on her skull-throne, next to Hades.

Demeter glided towards Persephone. She reached out to her.

'On one condition,' said Hades.

Then one of the palace gardeners began to hoot with laughter. The sound echoed right round Hades' palace. The gardener pointed at Persephone, he jabbed his forefinger into her rosy cheek.

'I saw her,' he hooted. 'In the orchard! She picked a pomegranate, and she ate seven seeds.'

Hades turned to Persephone, grinning. 'Is this true?' he said.

'Persephone, is it true?' cried Demeter.

'It is true,' said Persephone.

'You have eaten the food of the dead,' said Hades. 'You must stay in the underworld.'

*   *   *

Zeus took pity on Persephone. He took pity on Demeter, and on men, women and children suffering all over the earth, as far as the circular ocean that surrounds us all.

When he heard Persephone had eaten seven pomegranate seeds, he ruled she should pass three months of each year with Hades in the world of the dead and nine months with her mother in the world of the living.

Then Persephone and her mother left the underworld. They rose to the light in sowing-time. The larks sang descants and once more green blades grew from the rich red earth. Bushes burst into flames, orange petals, rose petals, crimson. The middle-world put on its coat of many colours.

Quiet in their houses, men and women ate honeycakes and drank barley-water flavoured with mint. They sipped sweet wine. They gave thanks for Persephone's return.

But Demeter never forgave the palace gardener. First she imprisoned him in an earth-hole, and then she turned him into a short-eared owl.

* * *

So the years pass. Each spring rain falls; each summer warm wind blesses the corn and barley; each autumn the harvest is brought home, white and gold. Each winter roots curl up, stalks turn black. Persephone moves from world to world.

ARTHUR THE KING

This falling snow is like an old man. It keeps forgetting itself, and wandering sideways. It doesn't really want to touch the ground. And now that the sun is shining, hazy, away in the west, the flakes look so frail you can almost see through them.

Sir Ector told me it was snowing when I was born. He said it was a fierce winter. Well, there have been many fierce winters since then: axe-winters, wolf-winters. There always will be.

Before my life ends, I want to describe my beginning—or, at least, the day that changed everything. I was twelve. So Kay, my elder brother, would have been six—no, seventeen. At any rate, I'm sure he had just been knighted, on All-Hallows' Day.

*   *   *

For several months after the death of King Uther—Uther Pendragon—the island of Britain had no king. True, Uther and Igraine, his queen, did have a son, but he had been entrusted to foster-parents when he was a baby, and only two people knew who they were: one was the old king himself, and he had gone to earth, like fallen snow; the other was the magician Merlin, and he wasn't telling.

When Uther died, everyone expected the foster-parents to claim the throne for their son, but this couple didn't realise they had the king's child in their care. So then the knights of the island began to talk and argue and lobby and squabble.

The Archbishop was worried. 'Our country needs a king,' he said, 'just as a king needs his fighting men and working men and praying men. We're like a ship without a rudder.'

Old Merlin agreed. He told the Archbishop to announce a tournament for New Year's Day, and then a great gathering at St Paul's, to choose the new king.

'Can I come?' I asked my father.

'You?' said Ector. 'I don't see why

not.'

Kay wrinkled up his nose.

'Be fair, Kay!' said Ector. 'He's twelve. It's time he got the feel of things.'

On our way through London to our father's house, we saw quite a crowd of people in St Paul's churchyard. Sir Brastias was there! And Sir Tristram! And several dozen Londoners.

They had all gathered round a marvel: close to the east wall of the cathedral, there was a square plinth of shining green marble. A huge anvil had been set into the marble, and stuck into the anvil was a great gleaming sword.

Round the marble there were letters of gold. I read them for myself:

WHOEVER PULLS THIS SWORD
FROM THIS STONE AND ANVIL
IS THE TRUE-BORN KING
OF ALL BRITAIN

My father walked round the plinth. 'Where has this come from, then?' he said.

'Damned if I know!' said Brastias.

He was copper-faced, and his nose was red.

'Well! What about it?' said my father.

'I can't move the damned thing,' said Brastias. 'How about you? How about it, King Ector?'

'How about King Kay?' said my brother.

Brastias looked at Kay and snorted. 'King Kay? King Kiss-curl, you mean! Never!'

First my father and then Kay stepped up on to the plinth and tried to pull the sword from the stone. But they couldn't do it. They couldn't move it a hair's breadth, and neither could any other knight who came to the churchyard.

I did wish I could try . . . But I wasn't a knight! I was only twelve.

*   *   *

Knights from moor and mountain, knights from marsh and fen: on New Year's morning, knights from all over the island armed themselves for the

109

tournament.

I helped Kay put on his padded jacket and breastplate and thigh-plates and greaves and metal boots and, last of all, his helmet.

My father's servants, meanwhile, groomed and saddled our horses and tied Ector's and Kay's colours to their lances.

Just before we reached the tournament fields outside the city walls, Kay stood up in his saddle.

'My sword!' he exclaimed, clutching his sheath. 'It's gone!'

'Gone?' said Ector.

'I've left it behind,' wailed Kay. And then he rounded on me. 'You dressed me! Surely you noticed!'

'I . . . I . . .'

'It's not his fault,' said Ector.

'Go and get it!' said Kay. 'I need it. Please!'

I didn't want to turn my back on the distant shouts and braying trumpets, but I didn't want to let Kay down either. This was his first fighting tournament, and you can't fight without a sword. So I wheeled round and galloped back into London.

But when I got to my father's house, there was no one there—all the servants had gone to the tournament. The door was locked; the windows were barred; I couldn't get in.

'What can I do?' I said. 'Kay must have a sword today.'

That was when I thought of the great gleaming blade: the sword in the stone.

I rode to the churchyard—there was nobody about; I tied my horse to the stile; I stepped up to the green marble plinth; I put my hand around the beautiful pommel, inlaid with precious stones.

Perhaps I was nervous, was I? Excited? What I remember now is such belief: a crowd of sparrows rushed across the churchyard, and I was confident and determined and joyous.

I scarcely had to pull the sword. It slid out of the anvil and flashed in the sunlight.

There was no time to waste! I galloped back to the tournament fields and gave the sword to my brother. He looked at it very carefully, then he looked at me, and his eyes brightened. I've seen that look of Kay's a hundred times. 'Father!' he called. 'Look at this!'

Ector came ambling over. 'You're back,' he said.

'Do you recognise it?' demanded Kay.

My father didn't say anything. He just stared at the sword.

'I'm the true-born king of all Britain,' crowed Kay.

'Where did you get that sword?' my father asked me.

'From the stone,' I replied. 'The house was locked and I couldn't get in; and Kay needs a sword for the tournament. It came out of the stone easily.'

'You?' said my father in a low voice. 'We're going back to the churchyard now.'

Kay and I weren't at all happy to be dragged away from the tournament, but there was nothing we could do about it. We had to turn our backs on all the excited hubbub, the brazen trumpets and the armed knights tilting

112

and riding their challenges. We had to follow our father back into London.

*   *   *

As soon as we reached the churchyard, Ector asked me to sheathe the sword in the anvil.

Then he stepped up on to the shining plinth and tried to pull it out. But he wasn't able to move the sword, not so much as a hair's breadth. So my father looked at me.

'Me!' said Kay. 'It's my turn!'

But Kay wasn't able to move the sword either.

I stepped up. I grasped the pommel. Lightly and fiercely I pulled, and the sword came hissing out of the anvil.

Then Ector got down on his knees on the damp earth, and he made Kay do the same. 'You're the true-born king of Britain,' he said.

'I'm not,' I said. 'I can't be.' And I helped Ector to his feet.

Ector looked at me. 'You're the king of this country,' he said. 'And I want all the knights, and the Archbishop, and

113

Merlin . . . I want them all to see this.'

*　　　*　　　*

Next morning, there was a great gathering at St Paul's.

'We are come here,' said the Archbishop, 'to choose our new king.'

There was uproar, of course, when Ector called out that I had already pulled the sword from the stone. I wasn't of royal blood, after all. I wasn't even a knight. And I was only twelve. What's more, several knights there hoped to be chosen king themselves— Sir Tristram, Sir Gareth, Sir Ulfius maybe. There was scarcely a man in the place who hadn't sold his support to one candidate or another.

'It's a trick!'

'It's witchcraft, my lord.'

'He's only a boy!'

'Prove it! Go on! Prove it!'

I can still hear them. I can hear the cathedral echoing with objections and arguments.

Then the Archbishop led us out of the west door and round to the plinth.

114

One by one, every knight present tried to wrench the sword out of the stone; but none of them could move it.

'Now the boy,' said the Archbishop. 'What's your name?'

'Arthur,' I said.

'Arthur,' repeated the Archbishop. 'Can you pull the sword from the stone?'

I remember old Merlin half-smiling, and again that joyous belief. So I pulled the sword out of the stone for the third time. Lightly and fiercely, I pulled it out.

All around me, the great men of Britain were getting down on their knee-bones, and the people of London were shouting 'God's will!' and 'Arthur!' and 'Long live King Arthur!'

'True-born king,' murmured the Archbishop.

'But how can I be?' I said.

'I will tell you, Arthur,' said Merlin. 'When King Uther—Uther Pendragon—entrusted his only son to foster-parents, only he and I knew who those foster-parents were . . .'

Next to me, Sir Ector was listening

intently. I can see his upturned pink face, and white hair.

'And those good people,' said Merlin, 'they never knew they had the king's own son in their care.' He paused, and half-smiled, and nodded at Ector.

Ector closed his kind old eyes, and sighed. 'Arthur,' he said, 'I am not your father. I never was. And your mother's not your mother; you're not of our blood...'

'Your father was King Uther,' said the old magician. 'Your mother was Igraine. You were given to Sir Ector when you were two days old.'

'Two days old,' said Ector, 'and the snow was falling.'

'Long live King Arthur!' said the Archbishop.

'Arthur!' shouted the knights.

'Arthur! The king!' cried the people of London.

116

NOTES ON THE STORIES

The Pied Piper of Hamelin—*Germany*
The earliest version of this legend says the Pied Piper visited Hamelin on two separate days in 1284, and led 130 children to Koppelberg where all but two (one blind and one dumb) went into the hill. My retelling, however, is based in structure and detail on Robert Browning's marvellous poem, in which the action is concentrated into a single day and only one boy is left outside the hill.

Browning ends his poem by referring to a tradition that descendants of the children of Hamelin settled in Transylvania—and it is true that a large band of young people is thought to have migrated east from Brunswick during the thirteenth century because of over-population. But it is also possible that this legend has its basis in the unhappy events of 1212, when twelve-year-old Nicholas of Cologne led 15,000 children out of north

Germany (including Hamelin) to join the disastrous Children's (Fourth) Crusade.

Godfather Death—*The Czech Republic*
Half the tales in this book bring together the inhabitants of two worlds (gods and giants, humans and underground people, humans and animals), and two of them are concerned with life and death. But unlike fierce, cold Hades, ruler of the underworld ('Persephone, Rising'), the figure of Death in this tale is far from terrifying. He is helpful as well as unavoidable, like some decent neighbour. What this tale says to me is 'Some folk die when they can't keep alive!' It says: treasure life, but accept death. And keep your sense of humour. After all, what is the alternative?

Recta and the Cow that Ran Dry—*Finland* The 'underground people' are about half the size of human beings. Most of them are well-to-do and most wear something red. They farm herds of sleek, white cattle. Rather like the 'hidden people' and the 'mound people' in other parts of Scandinavia, they are neither for nor against humans; but there are always rules to follow when one is dealing with the supernatural, and it is unwise or even dangerous to break them. So I would call this a tale about a girl, driven by need, paying the price of disrespect. It comes from northern Finland, and is set in the eighteenth century.

The Lady of Stavoren—*Netherlands*

Stavoren lies on the IJsselmeer (once the Zuider Zee) in the Dutch province of Friesland. It was once a great Hanseatic port, and its people were so rich they were known as 'the spoilt children of Stavoren'. But this story dates from the sixteenth century, when Stavoren had already gone into something of a decline as a result of shifting tidepatterns and regular flooding. The story is sometimes also known as 'Vrouwenzand' (Lady's

Sand).

Thor Goes Visiting—*Iceland* Thor the Thunderer, son of Odin, is the guardian of the gods. Many of the Norse myths describe his contests and fights with the giants of Utgard—and this is perhaps the best known of them, first written down by the great Icelander Snorri Sturluson (1179–1241). Thor's companion is Loki the Trickster, himself the son of two giants, and he enjoys seeing Thor worsted by the giant-king. Indeed, the point of the myth seems to be to poke fun at Thor's massive strength, and to show that physical strength is no match for magic. I first retold this story in *The Norse Myths* (Andrè Deutsch and Penguin) and have borrowed phrases from that retelling in making this new version.

The Ugly Duckling—*Denmark* 'The Ugly Duckling', with its deeply comforting message that suffering, stoically endured, ends in joy, is one of the best-known and most loved of the 156 stories written by Hans Christian Andersen. In making a new version, I have here and there referred to Erik Haugaard's fine translation (*The Complete Fairy Tales and Stories of Hans Andersen,* Victor Gollancz, London, 1974) as my guide, and have reduced the length of the original by just over one third.

The Army of Bears—*Switzerland* The brown bear is the heraldic animal of Berne and, in the city, there is a deep circular bear-pit (*Bärengraben*) in which bears have been kept since 1480. But did the bear-banner and bear-pit somehow give rise to this tale (as a way of explaining why Berne honours the bear), or did the story come first? Of its nature, legend is a tantalising mixture of the actual and the fantastic.

The tale contains memories of the old hostility between the Bernese and Burgundians, and perhaps of the decisive Battle of Laupen fought in

1339. The village of Orsières, on the way up to the Great St Bernard pass (the Kingdom of the Bears) derives its name from the French *ours*: bear.

With my Right Hand—*Belgium (Flemish)* Between 780 and 1070, the raiding, trading, colonising Vikings were much the most aggressive peoples in Europe. They overran Scotland, Ireland, half of England, Friesland, the north of France. A heartfelt line in the Anglo-Saxon litany goes 'A furore Normanorum, libera nos, Domine': from the fury of the Norsemen, Good Lord, deliver us.

One Norse myth tells how Tyr, the god of war, sacrifices his right hand (by putting it into the mouth of the wolf Fenrir); so the young stranger's act in chopping off his own hand should be understood as a godlike gesture, an act of the very greatest bravery. This story is a variant to the legend of Brabo the Giant.

Persephone, Rising—*Greece* Demeter means 'Earth-Mother': she is the goddess of vegetation and especially of the cornfield. Her daughter Persephone is the very force that grows within ears of wheat and barley, akin to Dylan Thomas' 'force that through the green fuse drives the flower'. This moving myth explains how seed corn has to go down into the earth, and die, in order to be born again. It was acted out as part of a sacred drama—a festival performed at the time of autumn sowing—at Eleusis, near Athens, two and a half thousand years ago.

Arthur the King—*Great Britain* The historical Arthur was a leader of the Britons (the Celts) who fought and won battles against the Saxons in the south-west or north-west of England early in the sixth century. But King Arthur has long since become the greatest of all British legendary heroes: medieval Romances about him survive in eleven European languages, and each age, including our own, remakes him in its own image. The first English version of this famous tale of how Arthur won the throne was written by Sir Thomas Malory in his *Le Morte D'Arthur* (1469–70) while he was a prisoner in Newgate Gaol.